DAYDREAMS

A Richard Jackson Book

DAYDREAMS

story and pictures by

DENYS CAZET

Orchard Books / New York

Orchard Books, A division of Franklin Watts, Inc.
387 Park Avenue South, New York, NY 10016

Manufactured in the United States of America. Printed by General Offset Company, Inc.
Bound by Horowitz / Rae. Book design by Mina Greenstein.
The text of this book is in 16 pt. Zapf International Medium. The illustrations are watercolor paintings,
reproduced in halftone.

10 9 8 7 6 5 4 3 2 1

Library of Congress Cataloging-in-Publication Data
Cazet, Denys. Daydreams / Denys Cazet. p. cm. "A Richard Jackson book"—Half t.p. Summary: The
children in Mrs. Williams's class find it hard to concentrate on a blustery day. ISBN 0-531-05881-6.
ISBN 0-531-08481-7 (lib. bdg.) [1. Attention—Fiction. 2. Schools—Fiction.] I. Title. PZ7.C2985Day
1991 [E]—dc20 89-48939 CIP AC

For Dan San Souci

Miss Williams loved her new class and the class loved her.

Each morning, almost all of them handed in their homework.

They tried their best on every lesson.
But sometimes, no matter how much they tried,
their minds seemed to flutter about . . . and drift away.

When Molly raised her hand to ask a question,
she stood up . . . and forgot it.

During the dinosaur project, Robert sat in his desk and growled.

At recess, right in front of the snack bar, Gloria froze solid.

After lunch, Manuel and Francis went to the library
to return the projector . . . and were gone for an hour.

Miss Williams sighed. "This seems to be a blustery day for daydreams."

She picked up a story book. "Now class, I want you to concentrate. Try your very best."

"Once upon a time . . ."

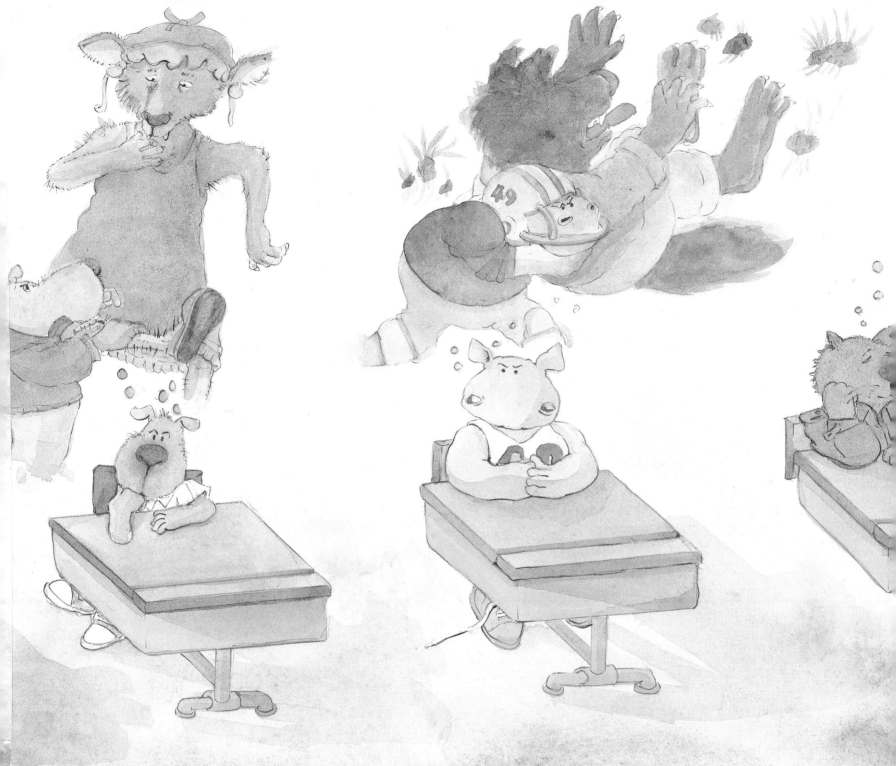

". . . and so, they lived happily ever after."

Miss Williams noticed Jack staring out the window.
"Daydreaming?" she asked.
"Just thinking," said Jack.

"Wishes and hopes travel with daydreams,"
Miss Williams said.
"On a motorcycle," said Jack.

The bell rang.

"Time to go home. Sweaters, jackets, books," Miss
Williams reminded. "And don't forget your homework."

The class marched down the hall and out the door.

They stopped at the curb.

Miss Williams smiled. "Thank you for waiting."
"My pleasure," said Bryan.

Miss Williams watched them, one by one,
climb onto the school bus.

"Wishes and hopes," thought Miss Williams.

"See you tomorrow, Miss Williams!"
"I'll be here," she said.